MW00573979

For all the kids finding out how special they are and how great they can be!

For my jewels, Zachary, Jessica and Jamie. For my family, Mickey, Perri-Anne, Michelle, Heather and Chuck, whose encouragement never faltered.
L.S.G.

To Andrea, who's learning to be great.
P.B.

NATIONAL LIBRARY OF CANADA CATALOGUING IN PUBLICATION DATA

Grossman, Linda Sky
Now I see how great I can be

(I'm a great little kid series)
Published in conjunction with Toronto Child Abuse Centre.
ISBN 1-896764-52-5 (bound).—ISBN 1-896764-46-0 (pbk.)

I. Self-esteem—Juvenile fiction. I. Bockus, Petra II. Toronto Child Abuse Centre. III. Title.
IV. Series: Grossman, Linda Sky. I'm a great little kid series.

PS8563.R65N69 2001   jC813'.6   C2001-902231-X
PZ7.G9084no 2001

Cover design: Stephanie Martin
Text design: Counterpunch/Peter Ross
Printed in Hong Kong, China

Toronto Child Abuse Centre gratefully acknowledges the support of the Ontario Trillium Foundation, which provided funding for the I'm A Great Little Kid project. Further funding was generously provided by TD Securities.

Second Story Press gratefully acknowledges the assistance of the Ontario Arts Council and the Canada Council for the Arts for our publishing program. We acknowledge the financial support of the Government of Canada through the Book Publishing Industry Development Program.

Published by
Second Story Press
720 Bathurst Street, Suite 301
Toronto, ON
M5S 2R4

www.secondstorypress.on.ca

Now I see How Great I can be

By Linda Sky Grossman

Illustrated by Petra Bockus

Second Story Press

Teddy, come here and play with me,

I'm as happy as *any* kid can be.

I have something important I want to tell,

Please listen to me so I don't have to yell!

Today I learned to do something new,

Because you're my friend, I'll share it with you.

Sharing makes things so much better,

Kind of like the feeling of my warm red sweater.

Teddy, a little patience, please!

I'll tell you for sure, I do not tease.

I found something out, I know it is true,

I'm very special, just like you!

The teacher gave us a project today,

But I couldn't do it, not me, no way!

So I thought to myself, "I just won't try,

He can't make me, I'll start to cry!"

"We're going to sew," is what he said,

And he gave us a needle and some thick blue thread.

"You hold the needle just like this,

Aim for the hole, no sweat if you miss."

He gave us some cloth and buttons and stuff,

Sam and Vesna got the hang of it, sure enough!

But no matter how I held that thing,

It seemed to be like a squiggly string.

So I broke my buttons, that's what I did,

To show them I'm a real cool kid.

"I'm tired of grown-ups telling me what to do,

Always saying, 'This will be good for you!'

But if I hide and pretend they're not there,

They won't do anything to me, they wouldn't dare!"

So I hid my head underneath my arm,

Usually that works just like a charm.

Teddy, know what happened after that?

The teacher came by and gave my head a pat.

He said, "Niron, I'm so proud of you,

You're taking some time and thinking it through!

If you need help, I'm your man,

I'm here to explain, if I can.

Threading a needle is hard to do,

It takes some practice, like tying a shoe."

I picked up the thread and gave it a try,

And another and another, 'til it was easy as pie.

The teacher said he was proud of me,

I'm proud too, of what I can be!

I can also help others if I try,

I like myself, is the reason why.

I know if I stop and think things through,

I can be helpful to friends like you!

And if some time I'm really in trouble,

I'll run to the teachers, on the double!

I know *they* will help me out,

No need for me to sit and pout!

I feel much better, being this way,

Because I can help in work and play.

I don't need to hide anymore,

Behaving that way was really a bore!

It's fun being special, don't you agree?

It makes me happy, like climbing a tree.

Teddy, thanks for being my friend,

And listening to me 'til the very end!

For Grown-ups

About Self-esteem

Self-esteem is a feeling of self-worth. It is how children "feel inside" about themselves. When children participate in activities that build on their strengths, it helps them to develop a sense of confidence and an appreciation of their abilities. Children who feel good about themselves are more likely to develop positive relationships and less likely to be mistreated in their interactions with others.

Parents can support their children to develop self-esteem:

Love them: Show children they are loved and accepted by expressing affection and spending time together.

Play with them: Create a safe, secure environment, encouraging children to explore the world around them.

Respect them: Have realistic expectations, fostering positive experiences and success.

Appreciate them: Accept children as individuals, reinforcing their strengths and abilities.

Talk with them: Use positive ways to guide their behavior, treating all children in the family fairly.